Max on His Tricycle by Guido van Genechten.
Translated from Dutch.
Original title: Max op de fiets

ISBN: 978 1 60537 004 0

Manufactured in China
First Edition
10 9 8 7 6 5 4 3 2 1

GUIDO VAN GENECHTEN

Max on His Tricycle

Clavis

NEW YORK

Look! It's Max with his new tricycle.
Max is very proud of his tricycle.
It has three wheels, two pedals, and handlebars.

But most impressive of all, is the horn.
Max honks it whenever he passes a friend.
"Toot! Toot!"

Look! It's Molly and Mary on their scooters.
"Toot! Toot!"
"Hello, Max," Molly and Mary call as they wave.
"What a beautiful tricycle!" they say.

Look!
Up ahead is Spike
on his tractor.
Max peddles faster.
Soon, he catches up
with Spike,
and then passes him.
"Toot! Toot!"
"Hi, Max," Spike calls.
"What a fast tricycle."

Look! It's Harold pulling
Squeak in a cart.
Max races towards his friends.
"Toot! Toot!"
"Toot! Toot!" Squeak repeats.

"Watch out, Max!"
Harold yells.
"There is a rock in the road."
But it's too late.
Max bumps into the rock
with his new tricycle.

Max crashes to the ground.
Harold rushes over to Max to see if he's hurt.
"I'm okay," Max says with tears in his eyes,
"but I'm worried about my new tricycle."

Luckily, the tricycle is fine.
The wheels still turn, the pedals still spin,
and the handlebars still steer.
"Toot! Toot!"
Phew! The horn still honks!
"Bye, Max! Be careful!" Max's friends say.